THE LONELY
CHRISTMAS TREE

written by
BRENT A. MARTHALLER

Tate Publishing *& Enterprises*

This title is also available as a Tate Out Loud product. Visit www.tatepublishing.com for more information.

Published by Tate Publishing & Enterprises, LLC
127 E. Trade Center Terrace | Mustang, Oklahoma 73064 USA
1.888.361.9473 | www.tatepublishing.com

Tate Publishing is committed to excellence in the publishing industry. The company reflects the philosophy established by the founders, based on Psalm 68:11,
"The Lord gave the word and great was the company of those who published it."

Book design copyright © 2011 by Tate Publishing, LLC. All rights reserved.
Cover and interior design by Chris Webb
Illustrations by Greg White

Published in the United States of America

ISBN: 978-1-61739-100-2
Juvenile Fiction / Religious / Christian / Holidays & Celebrations
11.01.26

"A mighty flame followeth a tiny spark."

—Dante

To my children and grandchildren
for your everlasting love.
May you all find that spark within yourselves.
Always look for the light.

When I was growing up, I knew the day would soon arrive.
They would come and cut me down, but I'd still be alive.

They'd haul me from this farm along with all the others too.
We'd be a part of Christmas; that's what we were meant to do.

They took us to the city and unloaded us that night.
And put us in a fence where they knew we'd be all right.

We stood there all together knowing that soon we would be,
Not like all of the others but someone's Christmas tree.

When morning came they tagged us and put us in a row.
We all looked around to see who'd be the first to go.

People came and went and many trees sold that day.
But no one really looked at me so I guess I had to stay.

I thought someone would want me, and so I felt sad.
But I'm not the only tree left so I don't feel too bad.

As the days went on and on, and more people passed me by,
I finally looked down at myself, and that's when I knew why.

My branches weren't the fullest; there were spaces in between.
I was only four feet tall, and I wasn't really green.

But inside I had the spirit, if only people knew,
To brighten up their Christmas; that's all I want to do.

Now everyone was leaving, and they pulled the fence away.
As I fell down to the ground, I heard someone say,

"Since you're the last one left, you might as well stay here.
Too bad you'll miss out on the Christmas fun this year."

There's a star shining in the heavens, and it's alone just like me.
Everyone picked all the others; I'm the lonely Christmas tree.

Though I'm not the best to look at, I'm more than what you see.
Oh, I wish someone would take me. I'm the lonely Christmas tree.

I lay there all alone and watched the snow fall from the sky.
I knew my dream had ended, and so I started to cry.

Then just like out of nowhere, a figure I did see.
It appeared to be a little boy walking up to me.

His clothes were torn and tattered with just stockings on his feet.
He asked if he could take me to his home just down the street.

I nodded, and I told him, "Please take me because I'm free.
I'd be more than happy to be your Christmas tree."

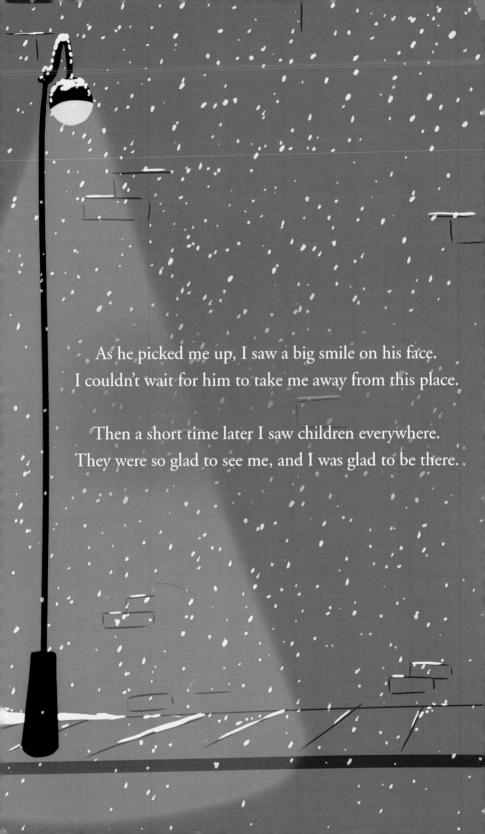

As he picked me up, I saw a big smile on his face.
I couldn't wait for him to take me away from this place.

Then a short time later I saw children everywhere.
They were so glad to see me, and I was glad to be there.

They shook off the dry needles and put me on a stand,
Then hung up decorations they all made by hand.

As they gathered around me and admired what they'd done,
I knew that I would finally be a part of Christmas fun.

There weren't any presents or gifts to pass around,
But we were all content with the happiness we had found.

These children didn't have much, but they all had me.
Now I don't remember being the lonely Christmas tree.

e|LIVE

listen|imagine|view|experience

AUDIO BOOK DOWNLOAD INCLUDED WITH THIS BOOK!

In your hands you hold a complete digital entertainment package. In addition to the paper version, you receive a free download of the audio version of this book. Simply use the code listed below when visiting our website. Once downloaded to your computer, you can listen to the book through your computer's speakers, burn it to an audio CD or save the file to your portable music device (such as Apple's popular iPod) and listen on the go!

How to get your free audio book digital download:

1. Visit www.tatepublishing.com and click on the e|LIVE logo on the home page.
2. Enter the following coupon code:
   30cb-2e9d-09ea-0041-71ab-a8d9-374d-8f28
3. Download the audio book from your e|LIVE digital locker and begin enjoying your new digital entertainment package today!